'Josie Gray's stories are modest, quirky, mischievious and unexpectedly beguiling. He has a sharp eye for the seemingly inconsequential, a proper sense that we make ourselves human by virtue of the stories we choose to tell.'

THEO DORGAN

'Reading *Barnacle Soup*, I was seized with the delightful and simultaneous impulse to clutch this book tightly to my chest, and yet also to share it with everyone I know. I'm so grateful to Josie Gray and Tess Gallagher for these intensely place-based stories of bright-burning souls.'

RICK BASS

for Victoria —
This will take to
the old sod!
Best,
Tess

4/19/08

BARNACLE SOUP

and other stories from
the west of Ireland

JOSIE GRAY
TESS GALLAGHER
LINOCUTS
ANNE M. ANDERSON

Tess Gallagher

EASTERN WASHINGTON
UNIVERSITY PRESS

Although actual persons, Mick Taheny, Tommy Flynn, Mattie Reagan and Josie McDermott (all deceased), as well as Mr and Mrs Michael Ewings, Josie Gray and his family members, are presented as they lived and spoke; all others, named or unnamed, are fictional, and any resemblance they may bear to known people or incidents is purely accidental and unintended.

Nonetheless, it is the special virtue of the fictional that it is able to transform 'reality' into its larger truths, and these stories are, in that dimension, 'true'.

JOSIE GRAY AND TESS GALLAGHER

First published in 2007 by Blackstaff Press, 4c Heron Wharf, Sydenham Business Park, Belfast BT3 9LE, with the assistance of the Arts Council of Northern Ireland.

Text © Josie Gray and Tess Gallagher, 2007
Linocuts © Anne M. Anderson, 2007
Design and typesetting © Blackstaff Press, 2007

Josie Gray and Tess Gallagher have asserted their rights under the Copyright, Design and Patents Act 1988 to be identified as the authors of this work.

Design by Dunbar Design
Typeset by IMD Typesetting and Design

First Eastern Washington University Press edition, 2008.

14 13 12 11 10 09 08   5 4 3 2 1

A CIP catalogue record for this book is available from the British Library.

For my family
and in memory of Madge

To the storytellers
and musicians of Ireland

JOSIE GRAY

For the spirits and friends of Ballindoon
who've sustained me for over thirty years.

For Tommy Flynn, who one day showed me
his headstone at Ballindoon Abbey with its little boat
, heading out toward Inishbeg and said,
'Isn't it fine, Tess? Isn't it fine?'

For Raymond Carver, who visited Ballindoon
with me in 1984, and whose love of a good story
encouraged me throughout.

TESS GALLAGHER

Contents

TESS
Why do you tell stories?

JOSIE
To see if anyone will listen.
And to get the story beyond listeners.

Keeping stories alive

Josie Gray, a County Sligo painter and father of eight, tells yarns with the same passion some men court beautiful women or bet on horses, although he's been known to do the latter as well.

From the time of our meeting in 1994, I have admired Josie's gentle, unpretentious way of allowing a story to simply unfold, no fuss or bother. I've tried to preserve, in these written forms, the reverberative power that struck me when I first heard these stories.

My initial attraction to the telling of stories probably goes back to those I listened to as a child, told by my maternal grandfather in the Missouri Ozarks. I listened to Josie as I did to my grandfather, with a child's heart, allowing myself to be swept away.

When, after two years of listening, I persuaded Josie to let me record a story or two into a little hand-held tape recorder, he wasn't pleased. Not only is it against the grain of an Irishman to repeat a story verbatim, it is virtually impossible to do so, for the story is always an ongoing act of imagination – no matter what its stimulus, or how it has been told in the past. It was also as if recording the story might be a breach of intimacy, because, on some level, the telling of a story is a form of courtship, whether of the listener or of the muse. But as Josie got used to the contraption, each story was simply spoken.

Our friend and my former secretary, Dorothy Catlett, deserves a lion's share of praise for transcribing the stories and then staying with the project throughout its many revisions. Josie would go over her transcriptions, add bits, answer queries and return them to me. I would then sort out melody lines, clarifying and cutting and rearranging, until the story had found its best music and meaning on the page. In doing so, I reinforced the nuances of Josie's voice, his rhythms and pacing – the emphasis he'd given aloud. I also added touches of my own, as the story invited, and as Josie agreed, for our way of working admitted the joining of two voices and imaginations at crucial points in the written form.

We gave special attention, for instance, to some endings of stories recreated for the page. Since the oral manner of passing out of a story can be a range of actions – a verbal shrug, mild laughter, a stoking of a fire, silence, or a deft bridging that runs one story seamlessly into the next – we had to do something else in the written versions.

The oral offhand slide or verbal comma often seemed not to satisfy in written form. Nonetheless, we allowed as many of the stories as we could to end as they'd been told. Others drift into whisper, break off unceremoniously, or settle in like the cat to the cushion. We felt free to encourage a telling to discover its written form, reorganising and embellishing for the page, allowing what Frank O'Connor has called 'fresh emphasis', and trying to achieve what Raymond Carver identified as the 'hum' a story makes when it is well told.

The story around this collection is that of two people, a teller and a writer, coming together from separate cultures, Irish and American, with complementary talents, to do something that could not have been done without the other. Still, I know I will have failed in the most part by having to leave behind the rare, incalculable stream from which I received these stories – the timbre of Josie's own beautifully registered and subtly nuanced voice.

I hope these stories may become, first of all, an enjoyment for the reader, as well as a lasting tribute to Josie's unpretentious love of giving stories – and to the faith we found, over twelve years together, to make this book.

But also, I offer these stories as encouragement to all those unsung storytellers in Ireland and America, probably one in every household. Keep telling those stories! And may we give them our own deep listening.

TESS GALLAGHER

THE BEST BLOOD
IN EUROPE

TESS
Do you need to tell the story?

JOSIE
Are you listening?

A hare on the chest

We were young and kept greyhounds, my brothers and I. We would hunt the wilds for hares every Sunday. We'd gather with two or three neighbours who had greyhounds, and we'd have little tests to see whose hound was the best.

On this particular day there were three hounds on the expedition, but one was kept on a leash. To set three dogs on one hare would be unsporting. The hares were usually in a field two hundred yards away and we used a little brown-and-white terrier to flush them out.

But in all the excitement this day, when the dogs were set loose, the third dog managed to pull his head out of the collar and took off with the others after the hare. Most of the time the hares would escape, because there were bushes and hedges and rocks, and they knew the terrain. But this time, with three dogs, it was tough.

We were standing in the gateway and saw the three dogs closing in on the hare. She kept twisting and turning in the field, back and forth. Her number was nearly up, but she headed for the gate where I was standing with my neighbours and, when the dogs were two feet behind her, she jumped straight up in the air and landed into the arms of the man standing next to me. And, of course, the dogs dodged wildly round and about, looking for her, confused as to how she could suddenly disappear into thin air while they still smelled her more than ever.

It was wintertime. We all wore heavy wool coats. My neighbour simply opened his coat front, shoved the hare inside, and buttoned it up again. Meanwhile, another fellow and myself put the three dogs back on their leashes.

So that's what the hare did. Jumped straight into the arms of her enemy – shuddering and quaking from her close scrape with the hounds. And she was spot on, because the man took pity on her, tucked her safely inside his greatcoat, turned and walked away up the field with her.

When my neighbour was well out of sight of the dogs, he unbuttoned his coat, and she sprang from his chest to the ground and tore through the field, back into her world – the world at the margins of our world.

The Elbow

Mrs McHugh couldn't straighten herself, so she went around looking down at the ground all her life, like a walking elbow. Eventually – it had to happen – she died.

In the corner of her kitchen, where they laid her out, there was what they call a *pooch*, a raised area with a nice fire close by. The mourners had to tie Mrs McHugh down with a rope so she flattened out, and when they finished, she did look lovely and flat. Then the relatives pulled over the curtain in the *pooch* for a bit of privacy and sat close up around the bed.

Just after dark, the wake of the Elbow was going

grand. There was the usual drinking, singing and storytelling about the deceased person's life. There she lay – like a queen of herself – and some of the people praying, and some telling lies. In front of the bed, six women were kneeling, saying the rosary, their eyes clamped shut and their heads leaning towards the flattened Elbow.

Right in the middle of it all, while the rosary was being said, this mad fellow takes out a razor, reaches in behind the headboard and cuts the rope. Suddenly the Elbow shoots straight up in the bed like a spring-loaded jack-in-the-box.

Most of the women left off their prayers and nearly fainted away, or ran out the door. Those bold creatures that stood their ground and had seen everything – they had to tie Mrs McHugh back down and wait for rigor mortis to set in properly.

Finally, when they were sure she was set like a plank, they went to the door and called to anyone who hadn't darted home across the meadows to come back into the kitchen, where the praying and lying and singing started up again with a vengeance.

And didn't the madman come around for a repeat performance! But when he slashed the rope this time, the Elbow refused to rise up.

There was no spring left to her. She was all stately and flat – maybe for the first time in twenty years.

The next day, when they put her down into the grave, the mourners were properly respectful, and kept their distance. They were a small bit afraid she might suddenly spring up. And this story is told, to this very day, when any crooked person is laid to rest.

Surrounded by weasels

Majors were scarce around Ireland those times, but in our area lived a man named Donnelly – Major Donnelly. He was a great man for shooting and fishing. Somebody said he'd had to live off the land in India, eating snakes, lizards and mongooses with the British Cavalry.

At home, a story went about that Major Donnelly was up in this bog that bordered our schoolyard. It was there, while he was out shooting pheasants one day, that the Major accidentally stepped on a weasel. And didn't the weasel put his tail in his mouth and make a whistle – a shrieky, spine-tearing whistle. In seconds the Major was surrounded by weasels!

The story scared the life out of us, my brothers and I. At school, we'd be kicking a football, and if it went out of bounds into the bog we'd all look at each other to see who would be sacrificed. If we went in, we might step on a weasel, and what would happen to us then? We'd heard that if you injured a weasel it would follow you to the ends of the earth to get revenge.

Even if you managed to make it home after harming or disrupting a weasel, we were told that it would squeeze through a mouse hole, leap for your jugular and, in no time flat, bore a hole in your neck, and suck the blood right out of you. After they heard that, some of the boys actually slept with towels cinched around their necks.

We believed it. Why wouldn't we? None of us had ever met a weasel in a bog. To this day I've never seen one, except in an encyclopedia. In later years we discovered, or were told, there were no such things as weasels in Ireland, except in stories told to children. What we had were stoats and pine martens, cousins to weasels in the rest of the world.

Besides being eager to suck children dry of their life's blood, weasels were crazy for rabbits. When they set out on the trail of one, the rabbit would run for a bit, then – when it saw a weasel was after it – the unfortunate creature would simply collapse with fright and wait for its doom.

That time the Major was surrounded by weasels – the story went – he fell into a panic. The place was lonely and bleak, and there was high vegetation. But the Major was lucky since he had a gun. He'd had no choice but to shoot his way out of this ring of weasels.

One of us, hearing this story, asked how many weasels there were? Whatever number of weasels it took to surround a man, we were told. Possibly twenty weasels, we decided, had surrounded the Major. He'd carried a belt of cartridges which allowed him to reload in no time. We could imagine him, desperate to escape, shooting his way out from those blood-hungry animals.

Somewhere along the line we were also educated about a weasel's funeral customs. If a weasel died or was run over by a car, there would be a massive funeral. Weasels from several miles around would gather to carry the corpse of their comrade across the road, with a whole rank of their kind following. And no matter what would be coming, this weasel cortège would not stop crossing the road.

If you were passing that way in your car, you would just have to pull to a halt and watch. If you were herding cattle, they might stampede in the opposite direction. You could be trampled. Or, if you were walking alone on the road and a weasel happened to glance at you, you could be hypnotised and find yourself marching along with them. There might be a line ahead of you ten yards long, and behind you as many.

The weasels would be holding each others' tails clenched in their mouths and keening through their little white teeth. You were to do the same – catch hold of the tail of the weasel in front of you and do your best not to disrupt the parade. Since you hadn't a tail, a few rushes would do for the weasel behind you to hold on to. It was bad luck to break a chain of weasels.

All the while, you'd be heading into the bog toward the weasel burial grounds. Deeper and deeper into the bog. There were boys taken like that into a weasel cortège and never seen again. But some came back. And it was them told us all about the weasels' respect for the dead.

The best blood in Europe

Mick Taheny came rambling to our house when we were kids going to school. He was one of those characters chiefly after a free cup of tea or, better yet, a meal. The food in his own house, at the back of a hill where he lived with two brothers and a sister, wasn't great. So he'd land at our house nearly every Sunday night.

He had schemes of one sort and another, and eventually he started 'doing the doctor' on us. He came up with a concoction. We called it Taheny's Bottle. Wherever he got the recipe, there was sulphur in it and baking soda, vinegar and God-alone-knows what else. But we, as children, *had* to take it. Our father believed in it.

You took a spoonful of it every morning for nine mornings, and it was supposed to clean your blood and leave you with the best blood in Europe. You'd know it was cleaning your blood because when you'd take off your socks at night, you'd smell the sulphur radiating out like you'd been walking on the coals of hell. The sulphur went down into your feet, and I don't know where the rest was going.

One time Taheny arrived in the early morning. I think it was Saturday because we were off from school. I saw him pacing our yard with his chin practically scraping the ground, and I was wondering what he was looking for. So I went to him and asked.

'I lost me bit of tobacco,' he said.

'Is it a big bit?' I asked, and started helping him look for it.

'Christ, childeen, it will never turn over McArthur's bread van,' he said.

Taheny worked breaking stones for the county council for awhile. He had a little hammer, rounded on both ends, and I can see him yet, sitting on a pile of stones with a bag of hay under him for a cushion, tipping away, smashing stones to fill holes in the road.

A few years later we got our chance to get back at Taheny for causing us such misery. This particular Sunday night we knew he would be coming to the house as usual. He didn't know our father and mother were away at the Galway races and weren't due home until late. So we decided to make a gigantic feed—three sausages, three rashers of bacon, and two eggs each – a smashing feed – when in comes Taheny.

He always had an old cap. It was never sitting on his head, but would stick up out of his back pocket, forever on the verge of some great escape. More's the wonder, he never seemed to lose it. But that night one of my brothers managed to steal it.

We asked him if he'd like a nice meal. *Oh God, he was ravenous. Oh, he hadn't eaten a bit right for a whole week.* 'Christ, childeen,' he said, 'put on a good feed!'

There were six of us children in the house. We went to it and pulled out the table, put the plates and knives and forks around. Pans were sizzling on the cooker. When the meal was nearly ready, we sat our guest at the head of the table.

For some reason Taheny was terrified of our

father and he'd always give a little leap whenever Father came into the kitchen. We knew he wouldn't want to get caught, pulling a smart one by causing children to engineer such a feast. So just when the meal was ready, one of us sneaked out the back and into the truck beside the kitchen window. They began flashing lights and slamming doors. The rest of us screamed and cried: 'Mammy and Daddy are coming!' Then we all ran upstairs like bad mice. Taheny nearly broke his neck lunging out the back door. He went tearing through the side garden like a mad bullock.

The minute he was gone, we came back to our plates and sat down like six hyenas at an antelope to have our meal.

As we cleaned up the kitchen, we were careful to leave one dirty plate on the table, with bits of sausages and rashers, and a scum of eggs. And we left Taheny's cap in a state of contemplation on the table beside the dirty plate.

Of course when my father came home late that night he spotted the cap. 'What the hell was Taheny doing at the table?' he said in such a roar we heard it upstairs. Somehow that roar must have reached Taheny, for the man didn't visit the house, I think, for six months. Meanwhile, we were getting sharper and more full of tricks every day, running from morning until nightfall on all that purified blood – the best blood in Europe.

A stray bullet and sick cattle

Because, as I said, majors were scarce in the locality, we decided to manufacture one. We called him 'the Major'. Major Donnelly never objected to the rise in rank of our Major, and could be heard calling him that himself on occasion. 'Good day, Major,' the Major would say. Maybe he liked having the company.

The Major's father was nicknamed the Miner and I don't know why, since he never worked so much as a day in a mine. The Major was known locally as a handyman. Everybody wanted him, because you wouldn't have to tell him what to do. Just let him alone and he'd see things to be done and do them, like cleaning the yard, or painting the side of the house. He was paid every night, and if you didn't pay him, you wouldn't have him.

In any case, the Major was an awful man for drinking, for as soon as he was paid, he'd go to the pub, and he'd drink that money. If he met a few people at the pub, you wouldn't see him the next day, no matter that you'd paid him. He'd be too sick. It was no wonder he was a good worker because, with all the days off he took, he only worked four and a half months of the year.

The Major was his own boss and he was very good to himself. People who needed his help used to go up and knock on his door, and if he didn't feel like working, he'd hide. Or he'd shout from upstairs, 'I'll be down in a minute!', then slip out a window at the back of the house and disappear. People had been known to go into his place afraid he might be dead, only to find the house empty, as if he'd just evaporated.

Anyway, the Major came working for us. Mattie Reagan also worked for us on a steady basis. But Mattie, unlike the Major, had given up the drink, for it had gotten Mattie into rows and scrapes before he came to us. He told me he was fighting a fellow one evening and the two of them *fought and fought until the two heads were as black as crows, and the strokes were like the swallows.* 'Who won the fight?' I asked. No one, not even Mattie, knew. Another time Mattie got belted out of a pub and was knocked to the ground. I asked if he knew who hit him. 'No,' he said. 'And I didn't want to know!' One round with whoever had done the damage was enough. He wasn't going to discover who it was and maybe get another such belt.

After that episode, Mattie gave up drink altogether. In two or three years he was a sensible human being. Still, he was always a bit touched in the head. But my father took him in and he lived in a little cabin at the back of our house.

When the Major used to get drunk, he'd come and slip into Mattie's cabin while he was out feeding the cows. It was handy, Mattie's little house against the bank. In winter Mattie would have a roaring fire down beside his bed, and this particular day, I remember, he had the coal fire blazing. When he came in for a rest, who did he find but the Major, snoring away in *his* bed, beside the fire.

Mattie said later, 'If a man can't come home to his own empty bed, what *can* he do on this wide earth?' As he didn't want to appear inhospitable that day, however, he looked around for a solution that would clear his bed without his having to outright tell the Major to leave. He happened to have a little stray bullet out of a .22 rifle, and he just walked over and dropped it into the fire. Then, quick as he could, he stepped out the door and around the corner to wait. The next thing, there was this ferocious bang. Sparks and smoke came out the door, as if the devil himself had landed. But it was only the Major, covered in soot. Mattie said, 'A swallow never came out a door as fast as the Major!'

Everybody liked Mattie Reagan. He'd go over to the lake looking at cattle nearby, and he'd chat Tommy Flynn – who hired out boats on the lake. If Mattie caught Tommy at home, he'd ask him to come stand on the road near the gate, to keep it open and then to shut it, so he could change cattle from one field to another. Mattie always called Tommy 'Mister Flynn'. So after Mister Flynn helped organise the cattle and had closed the gate after them, it would be Flynn's turn to seize his chance.

'Now, Mattie,' Tommy'd say, 'you'll give me a hand to teem a boat.' It was a five-minute job to drain water from a boat, but Mattie would look at the ground and answer him, 'Ohhh, Mister

Flynn, I'm not my own boss at all.' Mattie wouldn't help him one whit and would point over his shoulder at my father (his boss) in order to step shy of Tommy. It's true he didn't want to lift and turn boats and maybe hurt his back, but, more than that, he refused for sheer devilment.

Flynn had two cattle ailing one time. They were brought off Flynn's Island nearly on stretchers. Tommy called in two vets to examine these cattle to see what rare disease might be perplexing them. The boys were asking Flynn that night, at the rambling house, what the vets had to say about his sick cattle. Tommy started explaining how one vet said to give this bottle or that tonic. Mattie Reagan was standing behind these neighbours who were asking the questions.

The next thing, Mattie spoke up, bright as you please, 'Tell me, *Mister* Flynn, did they say nary a word about a wisp of hay?' – for island cattle were often in danger of over-grazing. It was a lot of trouble for anyone to take a boat to an island and carry hay to animals.

Nobody knows if any cattle languished or perished on Flynn's Island, but these ones at least had the benefit of Mattie Reagan's quick tongue that night.

An Irish solution

Tommy Flynn's cottage stood against a bank with a hill behind it. It was a beautiful little cottage really, but there was no running water and no toilet, except under the back hedge.

When a heavy rain came, it would rush in under the foundation at the back, then flow out Tommy's front door. He had three inches of water standing on the floor during one flood of a particular Saturday evening in April.

'What did you do?' we asked him. Tommy rubbed his hands together like a man before a good fire.

'Well, be-Jee, the first thing I did,' he said, 'was

to throw the spuds on the floor and wash them for Sunday's dinner!'

Another time, we were in the near-dark chatting Tommy at his cottage. He prided himself in showing off his shoes and boots, and his little green jacket – a jacket that wasn't actually big enough for him. He looked so comical, like a pea bursting its pod, squeezed into this little jacket. He'd have a green cap on to match, and blue trousers. He had a lot of clothes and he'd bring down the shoes and, to make certain you'd properly appreciate them, he'd say with a sober look, 'They *cosht* me *ten pounds*.'

Once he brought out these lovely leather boots with three inches of blue mould on them. He'd taken them from under his bed. You see, his house was a damp cave of a place.

Still, Tommy lived out his life there, going in and out of it, like a king. 'My cottage,' he'd say. And if he saw you passing he'd call, 'Come in, come in,' and in you'd go. He'd play you a tune or two on the fiddle and, between those walls that were nearly weeping with the damp, time would pass like the snap of a twig.

A FIDDLE
IN THE BOAT

TESS
What's the good of a story?

JOSIE
Just keep the fire going.
It's a bit of useless amusement.

A blind tongue

Tommy Flynn had a band. Its foremost member was Josie McDermott. Josie was born with very bad eyesight. I believe his father must have died when he was young, or at least I never heard mention of his father. Josie, in any case, was reared by his mother, a small woman who lived in a cottage at Coolmeen in County Sligo. Eventually the mother died, and Josie lived on in the cottage alone.

Josie's eyesight was getting worse and worse, but he kept learning instruments. Any wind instrument you could think of, Josie McDermott could play. He composed songs and was a lovely ballad singer. His songs were about local places and people, and he appeared on national television and radio singing and performing them. Actually, he became famous and there is a monument to him now in the village at Ballyfarnon in County Roscommon.

Josie eventually went stone blind. The disco scene came on for awhile and Tommy no longer had his band, but every Thursday night of the year Josie would land at another neighbour's, Michael Ewings's, and eventually he'd get into Michael's car and they'd drive out to Tommy Flynn's cottage on the shores of Lough Arrow. They would ramble there for a few hours – chat and maybe play a few tunes – then go home again.

This particular Thursday night, Josie had a button missing off his shirt, and before he left with Michael for Tommy's, he asked Mrs Ewings for a needle and thread. With the talk and all, she forgot to give it to him, so he landed out to Flynn's and had to ask him for a needle and thread. Flynn got them down, shook the dust from the spool, bit off a length of thread and started poking and stabbing, trying to put it through the eye of the needle. Failing at it, he began yapping and talking and fussing.

Then Michael Ewings says, 'Give it over to me.

I'll try it.' But he had the same problem. They were at it for ages. Josie could hear this carry-on and finally he says, 'Give me that needle and thread, you pair of blind bastards!' He stuck the needle in at one side of his mouth, then pushed the thread in at the other and closed his mouth on the lot. Seconds later he took out the needle, fully threaded. He'd done it all with his tongue. Next, he took the shirt to the needle and sewed on his button. He did everything by feel.

Josie's kitchen, I was told, was immaculate. All the neighbours who went in learning music from him said his entire cottage was immaculate as well. Everything in its proper place. But if anybody went into the kitchen to help him clean up, Josie would stop them immediately and send them out, because if they moved anything at all, afterwards he wouldn't know where the pan was, or the kettle. He had his little spot for everything, and he navigated by some intricate way a thing sat in his head next to this or that other thing. That's the way he kept the world.

Much earlier, when Josie was just a young fellow and his eyesight failing, he would walk home from rambling at night in some local house, accompanied by the neighbour boys. They knew Josie didn't want to admit how blind he was getting, so they often got up an act to cause him to misjudge the entrance to his driveway.

Yards before Josie's gate the neighbour boys would make a good show saying, 'Goodnight, Josie! Goodnight. See you tomorrow.' Then they would stand back a few paces and watch him step boldly off into the ditch. He would have to paw his way out and go the rest of the way home by a prayer and a guess. Such were the humours and delights of young boys.

Despite this, Josie never complained or shunned anyone or spoke badly of others. In this too, his tongue was far from blind.

A fiddle in the boat

Besides Josie McDermott, there was another neighbour who played the fiddle and was a genius. His name was Shane Coggins. He wasn't a permanent fixture in Tommy Flynn's band, but he played with them on occasion. Shane was a bit of a comedian. He would hop the bow two feet in the air off the strings, just for amusement.

I asked Tommy one time what kind of fiddle player was Shane Coggins. 'Ireland's greatest,' he said. 'That's provided there's no pressure. In competition or solo in a hall, he's useless.' Then he gave an example. 'Once we were up to Dublin to do a recording for television and Shane broke down. Couldn't get through it. But,' Tommy said, 'put him playing where there's no pressure and there's nobody in Ireland as good as him.'

A few days later I asked Shane what kind of a fiddle player was Tommy Flynn. 'Ah,' he said, 'sure, you wouldn't hear him behind a newspaper.'

We were with Shane at a football match down in Cavan one time, and after the match we were going into this hotel to have a few drinks. There was a guy outside, a complete stranger to us, playing what looked like a short wooden fiddle, a boy's fiddle. There was no varnish or shine to this pitiful instrument. He was sawing away at it with his hat on the footpath, expecting people to put money into it. But nobody was putting in anything.

We passed into the hotel, had the few drinks, and on the way out this guy was still torturing this excuse of a fiddle. At this stage I think there were two coins in the hat. 'Excuse me, sir,' Shane said. (He was very polite.) He took the fiddle off the man and started hopping the bow on it and in seconds we were surrounded by people, watching this man with a nice collar and tie playing this sorry-looking midget of a fiddle. The coins started hopping into the hat like snow.

After ten or fifteen minutes Shane handed the man back the fiddle and said, 'Thank you, sir,' tipped his hat and off we walked.

Shane Coggins was an athletic man. He could do the high jump. He'd tip over a six-foot bar like a bird. But, for some unknown reason, when the pressure was on Shane, he just couldn't do it – either play the fiddle or jump over a post. For, despite his skills, he was a shy man.

The more shy he was, the more he invented ways to distract people. One thing he would do with five or six men around, some smoking and some not – all of us short of matches – was to wait for one of us to put his cigarette into his mouth. Then Shane would reach his hand into the red-hot fire, lift out a glowing coal and hold it up to the man's cigarette, then drop the coal back into the fire. He wouldn't bother using tongs.

He was a popular man at weddings because he could sing and play just fine on such occasions. In fact, he seemed reserved for the times when the real focus was on somebody else. Wherever he went, he always carried his fiddle at the ready in an old, battered-looking black case.

One time I took him fishing on Lough Arrow and, since the fishing was slow, he decided he'd play for the fish. He hadn't a drink in him; he just took a notion. He stood upright in the boat with his fiddle under his chin and me at the oars.

I rowed from the neck of the Unchin River to Drumdoe, the full length of Lough Arrow, while Shane played one air after another. The dusk came and the dusk fell, and we forgot about catching fish. With the dipping of the oars in the water, so peaceful, pushing us along the lake to the music, I didn't care if the moon shone, or if we ever came ashore.

A mouse on the shoe

Two Drumshambo men usually came fishing two days a week on Lough Arrow every summer. One day they parked on Tommy Flynn's territory, in a field across from his door. It was raining, so they decided they'd go into Tommy's and have a chat. One was a retired bank manager, the other a retired grocer.

Tommy had a good fire going. The heat and fumes were building up in the room – it was terrible. They were talking away for ages, and the retired grocer had his legs crossed and happened to look down at the foot that was on the floor. There, on the toe of his shoe, sat a mouse, as

37

unconcerned as you please, chewing away at something. The grocer couldn't move his foot; he didn't want to disturb this little creature sitting there peacefully having his morsel. It would have been bad manners to move both the ground and the table out from under his guest.

Tommy's storage for food was a greatcoat he hung on the back of the kitchen door. Into its pockets he put his pound of butter and loaf of bread. So to make his tea all he had to do was stand up and reach in to take out the sugar. The butter was in another pocket. The eggs were nested somewhere else. That was his storage. He didn't realise a mouse could scuttle up the door frame into the coat and pilfer out the food, or snack on it where it was. Or if he realised, he may have thought fair play to any mouse industrious enough to brave that rotten coat, ridden over with spoilage and mildew.

John McKeever, the guy with the mouse on his foot, told me he had a bit of worry that the mouse might run straight up the inside leg of his trousers. Now this is the last thing a man wants, a mouse up his crotch. John kept a sharp lookout for any upward movement. But when the mouse had finished his sup, he took off across the floor and scampered up the door frame straight into the pocket of Tommy's makeshift larder.

Indeed, Tommy was not a great one for furniture. He ate his breakfast off the wing of the kitchen range. If he had a kitchen table, you'd be lucky to find it under piles of newspapers. He had two chairs, plus a rickety little wooden armchair where he held court. Against the wall was a long plank on legs where most people sat, if it wasn't crowded out with rods and reels and fishing tackle. There was a desk under the window with what he called the Visitors' Book, and he was very proud that people from all over the world had written their names in it, along with such comments as *Great fishing. Great stories from Tommy!*

He did possess one special piece of furniture – a mahogany sideboard – that he'd purchased at auction for a few pounds. He'd placed it, like the Ark of the Covenant, in the dark of his tiny unused parlour. Years later he had his house renovated, put new windows in and sturdy doors. Then he invited several of us down after work to help him bring his prized possession into the kitchen, where most of his visitors congregated. That's when we discovered the sideboard was going nowhere. It was a prisoner of the new, smaller, doorway.

Some of the boys suggested Flynn take the kitchen to the sideboard, which he thought a terrific idea, until he realised he'd have no chimney for the cooker. 'Be-Jee,' Tommy said, 'I'm like Tom Andy.' This was a neighbour of his who had spent all winter building a donkey cart in his kitchen only to discover, at the end of the day, that, despite removing the wheels and crib, he couldn't get it out the door. 'There he lived,' Tommy said, 'to the end of his days, cheek to jowl, like a donkey to his cart!'

Face wound

When I was ten years of age, my brother Brendan and I were sent off to confession. We had to walk two or three miles to the church on Saturday to tell our tales to the priest, then walk home.

We were on our way back from one of these sessions when, about a mile from the house, we came to a little wood where many of the trees had been cut. By then the grass had grown up over the stumps again, but the trees had been chopped with an axe from both sides, so there was a spike in the middle of each stump.

Naturally we decided to take a race through the

wood and, of course – Josie being Josie – I tripped on a low stump in the long grass and landed face down in the middle of another stump and split myself. From the forehead the gash ran past the inside corner of an eye and halfway down my cheek. Over seventy years later, the mark is still there.

I came out of the woods holding my hands in front of my face. I had no hanky, or if I did, it was saturated with blood. There was a woman walking down the road, and I was trying, as best I could, to hide the fact that I was hurt. Brendan was trotting along slightly ahead, shielding me from her view.

Anyway, she spotted me. She said, 'Did you cut your face, dearie?' She came up to me and began to look me over. She saw the big gash and got very alarmed. We stepped over a little bridge across a river and she brought me, with Brendan trailing behind, to a little shack.

In this dilapidated place, there was an old man named Dominick McDonough, and the woman seemed to know him. She wanted to wash my face and find something to wrap around it, but the only thing the man had was an old crumpled handkerchief which he took from his pocket. From the looks of it, it had been there for at least twenty years. When the woman took it to wash my face, I remember the smell of tobacco off it. It would have knocked down an ass.

I got my face washed with this man's handkerchief, soaked in water she dipped from the river. Nonetheless, the blood kept coming. The poor woman took her beautiful white silk scarf from around her neck and wrapped it around my head and face until I looked like a young Arab, then sent me on my way home.

When I came through the door, my mother ripped the scarf off and here was this deep gash across my face. A schoolmaster used to live with us at the time, and he had an old baby Ford. My mother and he decided to drive me to the doctor in Bettystown, four miles away.

Some time before, I had heard someone say that the doctor there was an awful man for drinking, that he was drunk at least half the time he was treating his patients. I prayed in the back of that car, harder than I ever prayed in my life, that he wouldn't be available.

When we landed, he wasn't to be had. So we headed for Ballinrobe, another six miles down the road, where there was another doctor. When we arrived, I saw this young fellow coming out of the office with his arm in a sling and I hoped, whatever happened to me, I could get my head put in a sling. It would be romantic looking and I felt I was sure to get sympathy for my injury if I had the right bandage.

This doctor stitched me up – fourteen stitches – one in the corner of my eye, and the others on the forehead, down into the middle of my cheek. I was a great topic of conversation after that, with a running commentary on my good luck not to have lost an eye.

I was off school for a while, but eventually the wound healed. Still, there was a jagged, wicked-looking scar. Granny used to tell me to put spit on it in the morning, a Fasting Spit – 'Spit on your finger and rub it into the wound,' she said, and eventually this would wear the scar away. I was spitting and rubbing every morning in front of the bathroom mirror, waiting for the cure to set in.

Once I healed up, I would play football up on the back ridge behind our house. But I started noticing that when I played or exercised, every bone in my body would get stiff and sore. One particular day I was so crippled I had to lie on my side at the top of the hill and roll down at least three or four hundred yards, all the way to the house. I simply could not walk, with the pain in my joints.

My parents brought doctors in to examine me and they could find nothing. I remember one doctor saying to me, 'I wish to God I had your heart. I can't see anything amiss with you.' So from that day on the teachers used to whack hell out of me because they reckoned I was putting on all this sickness.

One day I remember our class was told to dig weeds off the driveway approaching the school. I was glad to get working at this, so I took a spade and had done only a few minutes' work when the teacher came around the corner. She took the spade off me and clapped me two belts on the back of the ear with her hand. She said she didn't want me working the spade because I'd soon be grumbling and complaining about pain, for by then I had a reputation.

Eventually, I stopped growing entirely. A year and a half had passed since my tumble and I hadn't grown at all. In fact, I think I'd even shrunk a bit. I was hardly twelve years old.

One day a doctor who was always friendly with the family and knew my father, came into our house. This doctor used to drop in for a cup of tea and a chat, but this day he was brought down to the parlour to examine me. Doctor Delaney had me bending my knees and elbows, and of course, since I hadn't been exerting myself, everything was perfect. I didn't need any oil in the hinges.

For the first time in his life, my father happened to be beside me with the doctor, and my father said, 'Well I don't know what the hell is going on, but it's into the stage now where I can't sit down at the same dinner table as this boy.'

'Why?' said the doctor.

'Because,' said my father, 'he's always sniffling.'

The doctor took out a big contraption from his bag. 'Show me that nose,' he said. Then he spread my nostrils and looked up inside them. 'How did you get that cut on your face?' he asked. I told him I'd fallen on a stump. 'Well you have a shattered bone in your nose,' he said. 'Whatever doctor stitched that up should have sent you for an X-ray to make sure nothing was broken. You have a broken bone decaying away, poisoning your whole system.' He said, 'If you have that for another three or four months, you'll be in your grave, because it will set in gangrene. You'll have to go to Dublin now,' he said, 'and get that bone removed, because it's in a tricky place.'

At this time my father was in the oil business and I was sent up on this big oil lorry to Dublin and put in hospital. Eventually the morning of the operation arrived. The attendants brought me in and put this mask across my face and had me take deep breaths of ether. I went into fairyland. But I woke up in bed in the hospital, with nobody around that I knew.

Jesus, was I sick and mad with thirst! I called the nurses and they brought me in a little mug like a miniature teapot, with a spout on it. It was half filled with water. I had that drunk in seconds.

Jimmy Lane, the guy who drove the oil lorry, was back in Dublin for a second load and came up to see me. He brought me an orange and even peeled it for me, but I couldn't get it into my mouth. I squashed the segments through my teeth and managed to get some of the juice. I could not believe the ferocious thirst I had.

Finally, an old fellow beside me in the next bed – I don't know who he was or where he was from – called over this nurse. He said, 'This young fellow is dying with thirst and nobody gives him a decent drink. Will you look after him?'

The nurse went out and brought in a big jug full of water and left it down beside me. She handed me a big bowl. 'Now,' she said, 'after you drink this, you're going to get sick. The reason the nurses wouldn't give you much to drink was because you might burst the stitches in the roof of your mouth.'

The surgeon had taken the bone out through my mouth and they must have clamped my mouth wide open, because when it closed again, I couldn't open it. And so I needed the spout in order to drink. My jaws were locked and I could separate my teeth only a fraction.

With the jug of water beside me, the small pot and the bowl, I started drinking. I drank, and I drank, and I drank for a solid half-hour, the entire jug of water, taking it in through the spout of the small pot, again and again. Sure enough, I found myself getting sick and had to grab for the bowl. I didn't take a drink of water for six months after. I'd had enough. The terrible thirst was gone. Eventually the nose healed up, and the roof of my mouth healed, and I was home again.

Afterwards, when people noticed my scar, they would ask, 'What happened to you? How'd you get that?' They also began offering hints as to how I could get rid of it. I think somebody even told me to rub a black snail on it, but I didn't. Another remedy was that if you came across a stone where there happened to be a little dip full of water in it, to take that water on your finger and rub it across the scar. Another cure was to rub the scar with raw potato.

But I went on using only the spit-in-the-morning remedy, which you did first thing in the morning before eating. I would spit on my finger and rub it across the scar, then five minutes later I'd have to wash my face and the cure would be rinsed down the sink.

That scar has travelled everywhere with me by now. It still runs like a sword blade wound between my two eyes and down my cheek. I told my eldest grandson in America, who watches a lot of movies, that I was in a cavalry unit as a young man in Spain and got it in a duel over a Spanish woman.

Once I let a woman believe I got it from a German in a trench. Another time, I just said, 'What scar?' That woman took her finger and followed the scar down my face in a way I still remember. Scars are an encouragement to lies. I've carried mine so long, everything I say about it is nearly the truth.

A bad night for dogs

Many, many moons ago, when I was fifteen and driving my father's sand lorry, I had a little doggie named Dixon – a Kerry Blue. While I would be loading my lorry at the sand pit, Dixon would get down and chase rabbits and birds. But as soon as the engine started, he was up to the running board, on to the wing, the bonnet, and then up to the wooden platform on top of the cab where we kept the spare wheel. He'd sit there big as you please, everywhere I went. While I dumped the load, he'd go off again chasing rabbits and have a look at the countryside. But as soon as I'd start up, he'd land again, like he'd dropped out of the sky, on to his little perch.

That dog nearly drove half the dogs of the country mad. Whether they were jealous, or what – every house we passed, a dog would come charging out, and Dixon would just grin down at them yapping, as much as to say, *Nothing you can do about this!* He drove them all daft.

This particular night – it was late on a winter's evening – I was dispatched to town, for they had run short of cattle feed for the farmers at my father's shop. Dixon wasn't with me for this trip.

In the feed office there had been a little blonde woman who'd smiled at me, and maybe this smile threw me off, so I wasn't as observant as I should have been on my way home. It was rainy and misty. I remember passing a neighbour with a horse and cart who was also coming from town. A mile on from the cart, within three miles of home, this flash came out of a hedge. I couldn't see much in the dark, or hear any barking, because it was windy. I suddenly realised the flash was a dog. He'd charged straight under the back wheels, and my truck had gone over him. That was it. The end of his life.

About half a mile on, a similar thing happened. I was getting worried after this second dog. What was happening to me? Why all these crazy dogs?

What were people going to say to me in the morning? Two dead dogs. But I was only fifteen and I quickly forgot about it. There was nothing I could do. They'd just come out of nowhere, those dogs.

Then, at the crossroads close to our house, a third dog met his Waterloo. He just leapt out at the truck like he thought he could tear it to bits. Dixon had annoyed those dogs every week for months. They knew the noise of the truck and they would come tearing out. In the middle of the day you'd see them and could avoid them, or slow down. But at night, it was impossible.

The man with the horse and cart had been coming along the road behind me after I hit the dogs, one after the other. Not long after I'd passed him, his horse had reared up on its hind legs and gone berserk. That horse was so wild it nearly broke the shafts of the cart. The driver had to get down and take the horse near the bit and lead him along the road.

Then the man saw a dark patch in the road ahead, and when he got close enough he discovered a dead dog. The smell of the blood was driving the horse mad. The neighbour had to hold on to the horse with one hand and try to kick the dog clear of the road so they could pass.

He managed to get the horse settled down for another half mile when the same antics began again, the horse rising up in the air. He wondered *What's wrong this time?* He got down, took hold of the bridle, and saw there was another dark patch on the road. After a lot of walking and exertion he finally coaxed the horse past the second dead dog.

He was beginning to think it was a bad night for dogs when he came within a half mile of his own house. This time, since the disruption came at a crossroads, the horse at least had a place to manoeuvre. The mare took off, gave a wide circle to where the third dog was lying, then went for home at a ferocious trot.

Three dogs killed in the one night. The last one belonged to my next-door neighbour. The second one had been kind of mean. He always charged us in daylight and followed us half a mile down the road, yapping. I admit I didn't make a big effort to avoid him.

Three dogs dead in one night, and a horse terrified. I was waiting for all the neighbours to attack me with pitchforks at Mass the next morning. But I kept my mouth shut. I didn't say a thing about what had happened!

After Mass I met the neighbour who'd been

coming home in his cart. He whispered to me as we left the church, 'You done a real slaughter last night, a depredation! A *dep-re-dation*!' And I said, 'Thank you' – meaning I knew I deserved worse and was getting off light.

The neighbour never let on to anyone else, just mentioned it to me quietly. It was a dead subject after that. Not a word more. Just three dogs less in the locality.

I was realising today that those dogs were the only animals I ever killed, and I spent over sixty years driving. I killed them all in the one night, and spent the rest of sixty years not killing anything.

But it went out of my mind and I forgot about it.

A close appraisal

All the boys, including my brothers and me, were all dressed up of a certain Sunday night to go dancing, with the direct ambition of chasing women.

Tommy Flynn was doing an inspection of us. He looked at Tony, who had on a lovely double-breasted suit, and he said, 'Be-Jee, Tony, it's a lovely one. A lovely one.' Then he glanced over at Brendan, whose suit was single-breasted. 'Be-Jee, Brendan, yours is a grand one too. I don't know *which* of them is the best. You have me *pizzled*. But, be-Jee, they're *two* lovely ones.'

This was going on a long time, until it suddenly

dawned on them that Tommy wasn't passing comment on *my* suit. We talked on and the next while Tommy looked over at me and said, 'And be-Jee, Josie, you wore as many as *any* of them!', meaning my suit looked so bad I must have gone through as many suits as anyone in a lifetime. It was true I was always spilling things on my suits. My dependable way of getting a new one, without much expense, was to drink a few pints until I could imagine my suit was as grand as anybody's.

Tommy was mad for women. He began asking us, 'Be-Jee, do you boys *get* any women at these dances?' And of course we were bluffing, telling him we got *any amount of women. Any amount!* We allowed as how we often had to postpone some to the following week, we got so many.

'Be-Jee, I'll tell you what we'll do,' Tommy said. 'I'll play the fiddle and we'll get in a bit of food, and we'll bring some women in here to the cottage and have a party.'

So the boys had a meeting during the week and we decided we'd buy a couple of loaves of bread and pots of jam for the party. Brendan wanted ham and tomatoes, so Tommy said fine. To make a long story short, we had the night arranged. Flynn went to great pains and got dickied up in his little green jacket and red shoes.

A Scotsman visiting in the area, when I asked him if he'd ever met Tommy Flynn, said: 'I *did* meet him, and I'd love to have *two* of them on the mantelpiece!' Tommy was that kind of a wee-sheen, donnie little wisp of a thing.

Some of the locals gathered at Flynn's cottage that night, waiting for the women we'd promised to bring. Whatever the reason, the women didn't turn up, so Tommy began to give out to us. We'd made *no earthly effort*, he said, and further: we *weren't serious about a thing*. He even accused us of *not being fit to get women*, which hurt our pride no end.

There was nothing to do but arrange a second chance, so for two weeks we invited women. On the night, they landed in cars, and by foot, and travelled over from neighbouring counties. Some came twenty miles or more, and we left them down to Tommy, all to himself. Meanwhile, we were away in the pub.

That night Tommy Flynn wound up with twenty-two women, lined on stools around his dank cupboard of a kitchen, and himself sitting in the middle, like a little green bull's-eye. We'd filled Flynn's kitchen to the ceiling with women, and when we thought our point was made, we showed up, after midnight.

The whole time, Flynn was playing his fiddle. Twenty-two women, expecting a great, hilarious time, were crammed into Flynn's cramped cottage. Well, it was a complete and utter disaster! The women wouldn't look at us when we arrived. They accused us of fooling them.

'Either feasht or famine,' Tommy said, and waved his bow toward the women. Then he began to play and I never heard him play better.

A FOX AND
A ONE-LEGGED GOOSE

TESS
Where'd you get that story?

JOSIE
It told me itself as I was telling it.
How it was and how it wasn't.
And how it might have been.

A wheelbarrow on the bog

In the days when we burned turf more than coal, all the local farmers cut their own. There would always be a mad rush in the spring to get to the bog early for the sheer honour of it, because that meant you were indeed an industrious farmer – to have all your seeds and potatoes in before your neighbours, and to be down to the bog to cut turf, so as to ensure having a nice cheery fire in the coming winter.

Making tea was an important ritual of going on to the bog. If you once tasted bog tea, you'd die to have a cup of it ever after. Whether it was the black kettle the water was boiled in, or the water itself, drawn from a well and carried to the bog, or the scent of the heather rod the farmer used to lift the lid to see if the water was boiling, or the belch of smoke rising from the damp turf, mixing with the brew while it simmered – there was, and is, nothing to match the flavour of bog tea.

After the water was boiled, the farmer would throw in a fistful of loose black tea. If he was first to the bog, the other turf cutters would come to his fire to eat their lunches and get their tea. They'd each have a few boiled eggs and a cut or two of soda bread their wives had spread with motes of butter.

The farmer, minding his kettle, would pull it to the side on to some slower coals to let the tea draw. He'd throw in fists of sugar, and later, when the tea had drawn, pour in the milk. There was a spout on the kettle and he tipped it to fill each mug.

When the farmers had drunk their tea and eaten their lunch, they'd light their pipes, or take out cigarettes, or their tobacco to roll a smoke. Some hadn't anything but dandelion to puff on, but they'd offer it to the others and maybe get a gift of tobacco, from those who had it to give.

Trouble was sure to strike at teatime on the bog. If anyone in the countryside had a calamity during turf-cutting season, they knew where to find men to help them. The workers would sip their tea and squint toward a speck of a man, fields away, running in their direction. On one occasion they saw the speck pause at the crossroads, where he'd met the parish priest.

'What's up, Jimmy?' the priest asked.

'Nothing but the horns, Father,' said Jimmy and hurried along toward the turf cutters, who, when he reached them, had to put down their mugs and follow him to a bog hole to help rescue his best cow, which had fallen into the hole and was struggling, up to its horns in bog water.

The men snapped up bits of rope from the ties they used on their turf loads, and they worked these in under the cow and, after a lot of exertion, managed to pull the cow out safely. When the priest arrived, hoping to learn the meaning of the strange message delivered at the crossroads, Jimmy was wringing bog water from his shirt.

'Never you mind, Father,' he said. 'You won't be delivering last rites to *this* cow. She's been to Bog Hell and back, and you'll only confuse her if she gets a blessing out of it.'

The priest stared into the muck-filled hole, then at the poor exhausted creature panting beside it.

'Still and all, if any soul in the parish was as easily saved as that cow, I could leave off praying altogether,' he said, crossed himself, turned on his heel and carefully made his way off the bog.

There were many intricate discussions about wheelbarrows on the bogs. Since you had to push them, the design was a much-argued feature. If you made the shaft straight, you'd actually be pushing the load nearly into the ground. It would take an iron man to wheel such a barrow. When the right man made one, he'd put a bow in the shafts, which meant that the wheel would bounce along, nice and high over the ground.

One way of helping a wheelbarrow run smoothly was to lower it into the water at the bottom of the bog hole and leave it for the day. It would swell up and all the reluctance go out of it. You could push it all day and it wouldn't complain.

We learned our lesson about well-designed wheelbarrows once up at our uncle's when we went to help him with the turf. There was a fellow there who could put forty sods on to his wheelbarrow. But my brother and I, doing our best, only managed fifteen on to our barrows, because if we put on more, we wouldn't be able to budge them.

We thought we were hardy young fellows, for we'd been exercising with weights, but we couldn't compete with our uncle's workman, who was twice our age. When it came dinner time, this fellow had his barrow filled and hauled fifty times, and he sat down with us to eat, as if he'd been at little more than picking his teeth, while we were exhausted from half as many loads.

After our dinner, I said to myself, *I must try out his barrow.* It was sitting there with a terrible load still on it. So I went over and put my hands on to the shafts and lifted it. I'd no sooner pushed it a few feet when it began to run away in front of me. That's how I discovered the beauty of a properly made wheelbarrow.

There was a farmer down the way who went to the bog early in spring. About a hundred yards or so down from him, he saw his neighbour, Pat, had gotten there first. So he went over to Pat's fire and, as the water boiled for the tea, began to chat him. 'You have a new wheelbarrow, I see.'

'I have,' said Pat, 'and do you know, I made that out of me own head.'

The farmer took note of the long jaw on his neighbour and the wide span of his forehead, and said, 'You know, I believe you. And what's more, I'd safely say, there's the makings of another in it!'

A wild hand

Tommy Flynn had a neighbour who gave him dinner an occasional Sunday. She'd bring him in and sit him down at the family table. Her husband was a fruit wholesaler, and if they had a little box of bananas left after the day of selling, he'd bring it into the house and leave it in the entry to protect it from frost.

This particular night Tommy was babysitting for this couple. He decided to go up to check on the children, but on the way down the stairs he spotted the bananas, and was tempted. He took a banana, and brought it to his chair in front of the fire to eat it.

The couple had a Stanley range like his, but it was coal and turf they burned instead of oil. Tommy never sat to one side of a hearth. He'd sit square in front of it with a leg spread to each side of the fire, enjoying the warmth. He had false teeth, so after peeling the banana, he took out his teeth in order to eat it.

When the couple came home, the wife says to him, 'Fair play to you, Tommy, you've a great fire on.' Tommy looked up very sheepish like and said, 'Pity it oughtn't. There's thirty-six pounds' worth of teeth in that fire!'

When he'd taken out his false teeth to eat the banana, he'd had the skin and the false teeth in the same hand. Without thinking, he'd opened the door of the range and pegged all in.

Ever after, when the couple looked into the range, they thought they could see Tommy's false teeth still glowing among the coals, long into the darkest night.

A fox and
a one-legged goose

Doors, as a rule, in those days in Ireland were built small to cut down on draughts.

Tommy Flynn reminded us one day of the existence of a particularly inconvenient small door. He said a certain priest on a visit to a farmer had left his open umbrella in a hallway to dry.

After his visit, the priest got to his trap and pony without his umbrella and called back to the farmer to bring it out to him. Try as he would, the farmer couldn't manoeuvre that open umbrella through the doorway. The priest finally took mercy and came back for it himself, slipped the lever, collapsed the umbrella, and stepped through the bothersome doorway. Then, on the other side, he snapped the umbrella wide again, all in a split second.

'Say what you like,' the farmer told his neighbours afterwards, '*they* have the power!'

Priests in those days would go house to house, performing the stations. One in particular made a great show of walking wherever he went, putting out advance notice of his requirements. This priest had a ferocious appetite and, where most men might eat a portion of a chicken, he would devour the largest part of *two* chickens.

The family, on this occasion, had prepared the two required chickens for the priest's breakfast and, after the meal and the Mass – both performed in the kitchen – the farmer and the priest sat in a stupor of beatitude gazing out the open doorway. They saw geese and sheep, hens and chickens crowded into the yard.

The priest, trying to make a pleasantry, said, 'Tell me, does the fox give you any trouble in these parts?'

'Well now,' said the farmer, looking him in the eye, 'you're the first of the year yourself, Father.'

Word spread about the priest who devoured all

in his path. At one household, the farmer made sure he tore off a leg from the goose for himself, hot out of the oven, before it got to the table.

The priest arrived and sat down with the family to the meal. He ate in silence the entire time, helping himself from the crippled, one-legged goose. Finally he could restrain himself no further and commented that, in all his days ministering around Ireland, this was the first one-legged goose ever set before him.

'Oh, that's the going thing in these parts,' said the farmer, 'one-legged geese.'

And to prove how plentiful they were, he led the priest out into the farmyard. There he pointed to a goose that had pulled one leg up under its wing to stand on a dunkle. The priest suddenly produced his pony-whip from under his vestments and cracked it at the goose until, as if on command, she let down her missing leg, and began to strut back and forth on her two good legs.

'There, you see!' said the priest, proud of having commanded the truth from a goose.

'Father, that's mighty!' said the farmer. 'More's the pity you didn't crack your whip at the blaggard we had on the platter!'

A golden goose

Pat McCarrick was a grand old man really, but his whole face was disfigured. They'd taken his teeth out all at once and hit some nerve that caused his entire face to slump to the side. He'd spent years going around the countryside on his bicycle collecting tax rates, before I took over his job.

Coming on to Christmas, there was this woman up in a place called Knockroe, and she had a goose. One solitary goose. Pat saw it and decided he'd buy it from her. He was actually buying it to more or less help the woman pay her tax rate. So Pat paid her for the goose and the woman was able to pay her taxes with the money. Pat said he would collect the goose around Christmas Eve. That was OK, she said; she'd feed her up well until then.

In the meantime, the local guard, Joe Murphy, heard about the goose and up he goes to the woman.

'Ah,' she says, 'you're late. McCarrick bought that goose.'

'I know,' says Murphy. 'But I arranged with Pat that I am to get the goose. I've already paid him for it, so you're to give her to me.'

So she gave the policeman the goose and off he went. Three months later Pat was coming out of Ballyfarnon, having collected a lot of tax money in the village. It was late and he had a few little whiskeys on him. He rode his bicycle over this narrow, windy bridge, and as he reached the other side, a bright light was suddenly shone directly into his face. In his glee at having collected his money, Pat thought thieves had waylaid him. But it was Murphy, the goose-thieving policeman.

'I have to fine you, Pat McCarrick, for having no light on your bicycle. You're a danger to the public,' says Murphy. 'You'll have to appear in court.'

'I suppose I can't stop you from your bad work,'

Pat says. 'But if you fine me, I'll have you in court the same day for the price of the goose you stole from me.'

Nothing went into the book that night and the ticket was torn up on the spot, for Pat paid the fine he didn't get with the goose he didn't get. Afterwards, to cook Murphy's goose, once and for all, Pat told everyone in the countryside how he'd trumped Murphy on the bridge at Ballyfarnon.

Pat was a student of human nature. He had great schemes for getting people to pay their rates. Some who were well enough off would nonetheless drag along and not pay what they owed. One such man was out in the field working beside his neighbours in the next field. Pat stuck his head over the gate and shouted, 'Have you the rates for me? *They* all have paid. Only yourself – you're the last.' He embarrassed the man into reaching into his pocket there in the middle of his field, for he'd had the money all the while.

When I took over, I asked Pat to give me a hand at the fair since, when the farmers sold their cattle, they would also usually pay their rates, while the money was hot in their fists. I had a little office in the back of a pub that Pat had kept years before me. Some of these ratepayers, mind you, would need a dozen receipts, because they owned bits of land in several townlands.

That day this oldish man came in and Pat says to him, 'John Dolan, how are you doing?' Most people would only pay six months of the rate at a time, so Pat was sitting beside me and started tearing out the man's thirteen half-year receipts. 'That's six pounds,' he says to Dolan.

'But,' says Dolan, 'I'm paying *this man* the whole year's rate.' Pat nearly hit the ceiling.

'Goddamit,' Pat said, 'I was thirty years collecting rates from you and you never had a shilling. How the hell comes it you're paying the whole year's rates in a swoop to *this* man? You'd never pay more than a half-year's to me.'

The fact of the matter was that John Dolan had about twelve or fourteen children. During Pat's time they were around his feet and he had to feed them. But, by the time I came along, fifteen years had elapsed. The last of Dolan's children had emigrated to England and America and all over the place, and there was only himself and his wife left. Some of the family were probably sending money home as well.

So, from being a very poor man in Pat's time, Dolan became a nicely well-off man in mine. He was prepared to pay the full year's rates and not have some rate collector shouting across a field that he was late, or the last, or the one who couldn't or wouldn't pay up. Still and all, Dolan remembered what it was to squirm and took no pleasure seeing anyone cringe over taxes, which, as anyone can tell you, are nothing but an evil, and next door to death.

But back to the goose – I told Pat that if every household's taxes could be discharged by passing a goose house-to-house and letting the rate collector eat it for Christmas dinner, this would be an ideal solution.

Unfortunately no such arrangement was ever made in my time, and this kept us honing and plying the awful tools of our trade: pleading, wheedling, badgering and scheming – living day and night as nothing but an outright nuisance and a scourge to every household and parishioner in the locale.

The rate inspector

Brian Regan, another rate collector who had a hand in training me, would sometimes recommend that the county manager, Howard McCabe, run his red pencil through amounts in arrears and write 'Irrecoverable'.

Regan requested this for particular families whose rates had been in arrears for over a year. This would allow them to start off the following year with a clean slate, owing nothing. It was a merciful act, but it also let him concentrate on devilling those who surely could pay.

That spring, Regan had decided to scrub the rates for two small farmers who had big families.

He'd had to argue their cases before McCabe, the county manager, who wielded the red pen. Regan went to him and said, 'I don't think you'll ever get this money.'

Everything looked good for Regan getting his way, but just as McCabe was about to run his pen through the debt, he had second thoughts. 'I'll send out the rate inspector tomorrow to double check – just in case. I trust your judgment, Regan,' he said, 'but we'll just see about this, for the record.'

So the only thing Regan could do was visit the two small farmers, that very night, and tell them he'd put his job on the line in order to get them out of debt. He wanted to make sure that when the rate inspector called the following day, they wouldn't get pressured out beyond themselves and somehow agree to pay. He also wanted to make sure any valuables displayed around the kitchen – a lovely radio, for instance – would be out of sight.

The radio was mahogany, nicely finished with brass. Probably the farmer had gotten it as a present from somebody in America or England. Anyway, Regan put out the warning and the rate inspector, Dennis Sheridan, landed with Regan in tow the following day.

When they came into the kitchen Regan saw with some anxiety that the radio had not been moved, and Sawyer Flanagan, the farmer, was sitting at the table. His wife, Peggy, was going around the kitchen, nervously trying to make order. There were three or four kids in and out, and a child above the kitchen could be heard suffering with whooping cough – coughing, coughing, coughing.

Rate Inspector Sheridan was a big, strong, grey-haired man. When he'd be checking the rate collectors' books at his office he would never arrive on time. That's the one and only thing he didn't do right. He might be three hours late at the appointed centre where the rate collectors would take their books for checking.

When Sheridan did finally turn up at the centre, he'd sit down and go through the books with his red pencil, three or four times. Then he'd get up and walk around the chair, squinting down at the books all the while, to make sure he wasn't forgetting anything. Every page in the books would be marked, checked, double-checked, then triple-checked!

This day he made the farmer take down the pension book, the social welfare book, even the children's allowance books, and he says, '*Surely* you can pay this man three shillings a week!' He named some terribly small amount, anyway. And Sawyer began to sort of agree that, well indeed, he might.

'We *might* just manage it,' Sawyer said, and then he'd stare off into space.

But Regan was standing behind Sheridan, his superior, shaking his fists, making gestures and grimaces to Sawyer: *No! You can't. You can't pay anything!*

So the farmer would swerve back into hopelessness and allow as how he was *devastated* and *unable*, even for the smallest amount.

After three hours of this carry on, Sheridan and Regan eventually left the man's house. Sawyer hadn't, in the end, agreed. He'd been about to, but then he'd admitted he'd made promises like this before, 'But I fell down on them. And I'd probably fall down on this promise too – the good Lord help and forgive me.'

So they left the cottage, Sheridan and Regan, and began walking out across the field. There was not even a road to this house, Flanagan's circumstances were so desperate.

Regan says to the inspector, 'You're an awful bloody man. To spend three hours with that poor farmer, trying to get him to agree to pay a few shillings.'

'But you know,' Sheridan says, 'I'm glad he didn't agree to pay.'

'Well, it wasn't *your* fault he didn't agree to pay,' Regan said in disgust, as they clambered over a stone wall. 'You put your whole effort into trying to make sure that he *would* pay.'

'Yes,' Sheridan says. 'That's true. But I'm glad he didn't.'

Regan took Sheridan's few faults as a kind of blessing, as if he'd been handed the job of explaining someone beyond anyone's ken. 'The man was completely outside time. But he'd take up everybody else's time, checking and double-checking. Who'd want to see him coming? When he'd go on his holidays, they'd send out a young fellow in his place. He'd be there smack at three o'clock. And he'd be out the door at twenty past. Done. Finished!'

Regan was just as quick to point out that Sheridan wasn't a native of the parish. 'He came from another county,' Regan would say, if there seemed any doubt about the inspector being a feather from a strange nest.

Then, just when Regan saw his listeners might consider nothing more could be said on the subject of Sheridan, he opened the door on a final chapter. 'All I know is that he wound up a lollipop man in the end. He had a uniform, a hat and a stick, and he directed schoolchildren across the road. That was his old-age occupation: a lollipop man. He used this coloured stick for stopping traffic, and he'd step to the middle of the road and hold up the cars until the children crossed safely. He did this forty times every morning. He'd double-check and triple-check the path of every child who crossed that road.' Nothing was going to happen to a child with Sheridan on the job.

Then, as if neither he nor Sheridan would ever leave the scene of those three hours downstairs from Sawyer Flanagan's sick child, Regan would say to me, 'It was beyond belief, the coughing of that child in the bed above. Where was the lollipop man *then*? Letting a father squirm for hours with his child a rack of misery over his head.'

And Regan would shake his head and say again how afraid he'd been that Sawyer Flanagan would agree to try to pay when he couldn't, when there was no way in a dozen lifetimes he'd manage it.

And hadn't they agreed, he and Flanagan, the night before, that this was the case?

Where, indeed, had Dennis Sheridan's eye gone that day but directly to the mahogany radio Flanagan had forgotten to hide. Still, Sheridan had strangely said nothing about it. To make things worse, Sawyer had turned on the radio just as Sheridan was leaving, and what came out of it but the Galway races – horses sweating under the whip, necks stretched for home.

A BEAUTIFUL
SINGER

TESS
Tell me the one about the beautiful singer.

JOSIE
What one was that?

TESS
About the thief who was never caught.

JOSIE
Ahhh – he was a bit of a storyteller.

A lake in the boat

In the early nineties, our minister for fisheries caused consternation in the locality. He decided that everybody in Ireland who fished for trout or salmon would have to buy a licence. Some said yes to him, but more said no, *definitely* not.

A few locals got help from fellows over in Galway and elsewhere to march against the licensing fee, and soon boats were tied up at docks, and the hotels and guest houses were closed. Then these same locals and their interlopers started to lay down rules for the rest of us on the lake.

Quite a number of us made up our minds that shutting down hotels and depriving ourselves of fishing wasn't the way to make our point. We decided to fish, and if we were caught and fined, so be it. We were going to fish without a licence.

So it wound up that, after a couple of weeks of this, you wouldn't know who your neighbour was, or your friend, because we were all looking the opposite way when we'd meet on the water. I fished this way for two entire years, and so did most of the neighbours – fished as if I was the only fisherman on the lake. When I saw another fisherman, I took care *not* to see him, and they did the same favour to me.

During the dispute, I was out on the lake acting gillie with two Englishmen when, in the distance, I saw a speedboat going from boat to boat.

'Have you got a licence to fish?' I asked the two English guys with me.

'No,' they said.

'Well,' I said, 'in that case we're going picking flies for a couple of minutes.'

So I put the boat in on shore, got out carrying a small wooden box and pushed my head into a bush, looking for flies. One Englishman said, 'Why are we picking flies? We're using artificial flies.'

'We're just going through the motions,' I said. 'That speedboat is the bailiff's. If we stay on the water, we're going to get asked for licences and be fined.'

Sure enough, the speedboat passed our territory and disappeared. Then we took to the lake, fishing again. I think we caught ten trout that particular day.

Sometime later, the fellows who'd turned their boats upside down on the shore followed our example and started to sneak on to the lake in the evenings. It's wonderful how contagious good sense is.

I was out this night fishing and I heard somebody shouting. At first I said to myself: *That's a farmer chasing his cows.*

Then there were more shouts, but I still didn't pass any heed. I had just put down the rod and given my engine a pull to start home when I heard a shout again, from inside a reed bed.

So, using my oar, I worked my way in to see what the matter was. There, thrashing around in the dark, was one of the guys who was totally against us fishing at all.

'I'm into a huge big trout here,' he said in a panic, 'and I can't land him. Maybe you'll give me a hand.'

'OK,' I said, and I began to manoeuvre my boat deeper inside the reed bed.

Mind you, this man had found it hard to speak to me weeks before. But I pulled my boat over and went to step into his. 'By God,' I said, 'this boat is half-full of water!'

'It's all right,' he said. 'It won't sink.' He had a small black-and-white terrier with him, and as I stepped into his boat, the terrier shot like a bullet into mine.

There was a fair breeze that night, and my boat drifted away with the dog sitting like a strange wizened creature in the bow, looking back as if to say, I'm well out of *this*!

I said to the man, 'I think you have this fish foul-hooked.' No, he didn't think so.

We had only a little tin flashlamp and couldn't see. Finally I heard a boat coming down the lake and I waved the pitiful lamp. It happened to be my son, David. He pulled in with a big lamp, which he gave to us, but he wouldn't stay.

I pointed the light down into the water and, sure enough, I saw this trout of about five pounds foul-hooked, running back and forth with the hook stuck in his back like the handle on a teacup.

The man said, 'Well now, there's a pint in this for you, if you can land him for me.'

Eventually, when I did land him, I said, 'You'll have to kill him or he'll jump out again, because there's a lake in this boat.'

The man took up what we call 'the priest' – a short length of wood with a grip for your hand and a knob on the heavy end. He gave the fish a crack to the back of its neck and dropped it on to the seat, where it gave a few wriggles and slid flatly off into the water at the bottom of the boat.

After that, we went to look for my boat, but it was dark and, even with the bigger light, we couldn't see anything. The boat had drifted in behind an island of reeds. It took a good twenty minutes to locate it, and when we did, there was the dog, still sitting on the bow like a little judge, not a bit fussed to see us. I pulled the two boats together and stepped back into mine and, at the same time, the dog leaped back into the other. Off we each headed home.

A fortnight later, in the local pub, here comes the man I'd helped, in for a few drinks with his wife. So I said to myself, *I'll test him out.* I went to where he sat on the stool and said, 'Well, any big fish since?'

'No,' he said. And no pint, either, I noticed,

which was OK, as it would have put me into an awkward bargain, to let him think he'd paid for something any fisherman would naturally do for another.

But I noticed after that how this particular fellow seemed to have lost his luck entirely. He couldn't catch a fish, not even by foul-hooking it.

I'd pass him on the lake and see his little dog, staring forlornly out like he didn't know what he'd done to get this strange assignment, floating around a lake in a boat half-full of water, with a fellow who couldn't land his own fish and who, if his engine died and he called for help, might drift through the dark until dawn before anyone would take the trouble to haul him in.

Offspring

The priest had given a great sermon that morning on the Blessed Virgin, the Mother of God, at Ballinafad Church. He'd gone on and on about her. We all came out from Mass and, as usual, people congregated around the gate and began to talk about the weather, the price of cattle, the state of the crops, and who had died during the week.

But Tommy Flynn stood with his hands in his nice green jacket pockets and studied this shrewd-looking fellow, not much bigger than himself, that he'd known forever and said to the man, 'What did you think of the sermon?'

'Arraugh –' said the man, 'he had a lot to say about the Mother of God. My mother was as good as ever *she* was, and there was no word about *her*.'

Tommy looked the man up and down, then gave a nod and said, 'Well, you could be right about the mothers. But there's an *al*-mighty difference in the two sons.'

The following Sunday the same priest's sermon was about money. He wanted to persuade the parishioners to increase their donations. He confessed he was finding it hard to exist on the small amount he was getting, and apologised for the fact that he had to ask. Then he went into great detail, explaining that it had cost his parents one thousand pounds or more to prepare him for the priesthood.

Later that evening he went for a walk, feeling very satisfied and hopeful about his morning's work. Along the road he met one of his retired parishioners, a man in his seventies, and he asked, 'Jimmy, what did you think of my sermon this morning?'

'To tell you the truth, Father, I wasn't at Mass at all this morning,' Jimmy said.

'Well, so you know nothing then about my sermon?'

'I did hear the boys discussing it in the pub after Mass.'

'And what conclusion did they come to?' asked the priest.

'Well, they agreed that a cheaper priest would do us just fine in this little parish.'

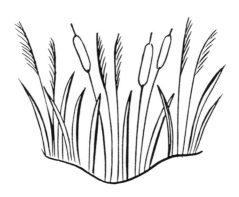

A beautiful singer

I was fourteen years of age and driving a truck in my father's fruit business. It was wartime, people were poor, and there were few vehicles in our locality – no cars or lorries – so we got into the habit of carrying people with us. We took them to town and we brought them home. We carried them here, there and everywhere. And for years after, I still found it hard to pass up anybody along the road.

Eventually, I married and was rearing a family when I happened to be driving in the south of Ireland and saw a young man thumbing a lift, so I stopped for him. He told me he was 'a man of the road'. In other words, he travelled and lived off social welfare, making good money, collecting it wherever he set his feet down. I gave him a lift, and it was a breezy, windy day.

I said to him, 'Do you walk everywhere?'

'Ah, but no,' he said, 'I have a bicycle in Kilkenny.'

'Well,' I said, 'today wouldn't be a good day, cycling against the wind.'

'Ah,' he said, 'but I wouldn't cycle *against* the wind. Whatever way the wind is blowing, *that's* the way I would go.'

It was like talking to some wizened spirit at large in the world, sent to teach me a bit of a lesson, for I never forgot his strange advice, and later I had occasion to make good use of it.

Years after, I was coming down from Dublin with a load of fruit, driving this old army wreck of a lorry that nearly drove me into a mental home. After breaking down by the road several times the same day, I finally got on my way home past midnight. By then it was raining and I saw a man standing on a bridge with a bicycle leaning beside him. He had his hand up waving, so I stopped. He went around, lifted his bicycle on top of the load and tied it down, then got in and we set off.

He was all talk. When we came to cross the

river, he asked, like someone coming on to a miracle, 'Is *that* the River Shannon?'

'It is,' I said. And he started to sing and yodel 'Where the River Shannon Flows'. He was an exceptionally good yodeller.

He told me he came from Kilkenny city and was on his way to Bundoran. He also told me he was a mechanic. My cripple of a lorry gave a little knock at one point and I had to get out to take a look, but this lad hadn't a clue what was wrong with it. He never left the cab. That made me cautious of him. I said to myself, *This guy is no mechanic. He's a chancer.*

When I came to Carrick, I was to knock on the door of a boarding house where my brother Kevin stayed and where I hoped he would make room for me in his bed, so I could get some sleep and continue my journey home in the morning. I gave fair warning to the hitchhiker that I was only going as far as Carrick.

But when we reached the town he said, 'I hope you can get me into the house with you, even if I have to sleep on the floor for a couple hours. It's too dark to cycle now.'

'There's no hope of that,' I said. 'I might not get in myself.'

'Well, ask your brother,' the traveller said,

'maybe *he'll* let me in.' He was getting pushy at this stage. When I climbed down from the lorry to take my leave of him, he suddenly said: 'Do you mind if *I* run up and ask your brother?'

Before I could answer, the hitchhiker ran past me up the stairs. By the time I came in with my case, Kevin had gotten up and gone for work. He was on duty from three o'clock in the morning at the post office.

It was still dark, but when I got to Kevin's room I could make out the shape of someone in the bed. Kevin had allowed the hitchhiker to get into his bed, the same bed I was to sleep in, and I wasn't a bit happy. There was the yodeller, snuggled like a suckling pig into the warm place my brother had just left.

I had a wallet with about thirty quid in it, which at the time was a lot of money. So I slept out what was left of the night with my head on top of the pillow and the wallet in my fist under it, to make sure the traveller didn't make off with it.

I got up early and left the singer still in bed. When I came down, the woman of the house was getting breakfast for me. The next thing, this apparition appeared with a big white shirt on him. He sat down and she gave it a cup of coffee.

I don't think he ordered a breakfast, as he probably couldn't have paid for it.

'Do you mind if I sleep on for a couple hours?' he asked the woman, all sweetness and charm. 'Well,' she said, 'I suppose that's OK.' He was worried about his bicycle, so the landlady said she would push it into the hall and leave it there for him.

I went off about my business, the singer went back to bed, and the landlady went to doing whatever she was doing. About twelve o'clock as she was passing through the hall, she noticed the bicycle was gone. She checked upstairs and sure enough, the interloper was missing as well, so she never gave it another thought.

This was a Friday morning, and there happened to be a social in the town hall that night. After a hard week's work, the boys came home and went upstairs to dress for it. Then the craic started. One fellow's suit wasn't to be had and another's shirts were missing. Ties were gone and jumpers, socks and shoes. He'd cleaned out the lot. I, of course, knew nothing about this, but a week later I happened to be ringing Kevin.

'You'd better not stick your nose back in Carrick for awhile,' he told me.

'Why?' I asked.

'That guy you brought into the house – ,' he said.

'Hold on a minute,' I said. 'I didn't bring him *in*. I *carried* him there. *You* let him *in*.'

'Well,' my brother said, 'he stole round and about him.'

The guards were called to the scene, and in a week or two they claimed to have their man. But the fellow they accused was later found to have been in jail during that time, so they had the wrong man.

I never could understand why they couldn't catch the fellow. I could have described him, how he could yodel and sing and had said he was a mechanic. But nobody asked me.

It so happened I was going back for a load a fortnight later and, as I was passing through Mullingar, this guy put up his hand. But I flew past him. Then I thought, *I think I know him*. So I stopped the truck a few yards down the road and the fellow came running and climbed in. He happened to be a Donegal man who'd also been hauling fruit. His lorry was broken down, so he was going to Dublin to do a bit of business.

'You noticed I wasn't going to carry you,' I said.

'That's right,' he said. 'I thought you were gone.' So I told him the story about the guy who stole all around him, the singing would-be mechanic with a bicycle.

'Well,' he said, 'Let me describe him to you.' Then he told me, in great detail, everything about the guy. 'He was blond, with a bit of a moustache clinging to his lip, pale-faced, about five-foot-nine. A swaggy sort of fellow.'

'How do you know all that?' I asked.

'I carried that fellow from Bundoran last Sunday night,' he said. 'When I came out from the dance on my way to Dublin, this very fellow asked if I'd give him a lift, so I carried him the whole way back to Dublin. He told me he was a mechanic.'

'Whatever he was wearing when you saw him,' I said, 'probably belonged to the Carrick boys. He came out of that town fat as a caterpillar in other people's clothes.'

The nearest the police ever got to the singer was when someone reported having seen him passing through a village with a bundle of clothes heaped on the front of a bicycle. Even then, he was singing, and the song was 'Four Roads to Glenamaddy'.

Every time I hear some fellow yodelling now, on television or radio, or when anyone sings 'Where the River Shannon Flows', I think of that bold hitchhiker. He's long out of my life, and the stolen clothes are surely rags by now. He's likely fingered closets all over the West. I do believe now he'd stolen that bicycle, and that's why he didn't want to leave it outside the woman's door.

Curse or gift, he probably just couldn't help himself, whether it was nicking other people's things or letting song pour out into the hearts of strangers.

A genius of a dog

Sam was a golden Labrador and he belonged to my daughter Miriam. When he was a little bundle of fluff, we brought him over along the lake shore, and he was so small that if he tripped over the least little stone, he'd fall on his snout. I was trying to encourage him to go into the water, but he wouldn't.

It might have been two weeks later or so, we went to the lake side again, and this time he was anxious, jumping into the water and scratching around. Miriam took a stick and said to me, 'You throw it out and see if he follows.' The stick was such a big one, I decided he couldn't carry it, so I broke it across my knee and pegged half of it out. But the dog didn't move.

Miriam said, 'You didn't have him smell it.'

I had the other half in my hand, so I gave him the smell of the remaining half of the stick and pegged it out. Off he goes, swimming. And he didn't come back until he'd got the two halves of the stick and carried them in.

Miriam had one problem with Sam. He was inclined to rove, and roving in a city or a town is highly dangerous for a dog. He came back one time with pellets in him.

Where the train comes into town there is a deep cut with a bridge at the end of it. So this woman was telling Miriam she was standing on the bridge and she stopped to watch. There were about twenty kids playing on the embankment, and she said, 'Your little dog was in the middle of them. Playing with them.' Then the train came, kind of suddenly, with a big blast of its horn. The woman said all the kids ran up the bank to get away, but one small child slipped and fell on the embankment, which sloped steeply toward the track. She said, 'Your dog went over, caught the child by the collar of its coat, and laid down beside it. He held on to that child until the train passed. Then let it go.'

Sam was able to open doors. He would just put his paw up and pull the handle down. So I said to Miriam, 'It's not good, that dog opening doors and letting all the heat of the house out.' I said, 'If he's smart enough to open them, get him to close them after him.' So she said, 'I bet you in five minutes I'll train him to close the doors.'

She got up and let Sam watch her. She opened the door and came in through it and closed it behind her. Then she pushed her hand against it to show him how to close it. Next she put Sam out and he opened it. She said, 'Close it.' The dog looked at her, put his head up against the door and pushed it shut. Sometimes if he couldn't close the door with his head, he'd put the two big paws up and push it shut. Any time after, if we told him to close the door, he'd do it.

I used to have to shout at Malcolm, one of my sons, in the morning to get him out of bed. He used to take Sam shooting. At this stage the dog was two years old or so. Sam would be anxious to get Malcolm out of bed so he could go hunting. I wanted to get him out of bed too, hoping to put him to work helping me.

Malcolm had this habit of leaving his trousers on the radiator in the room. Anyway, at noon this day, the dog went into the room, grabbed the trousers, jumped into the bed, and shot the trousers into Malcolm's face, as if to say, *Get out!*

Sam was even trained to bring back his own tin of dog food from the shop down the road. He wouldn't leave the shop until he got the dog food in his mouth. Then he'd head back to the road and trot the quarter of a mile home.

In the shop there was an Alsatian that barked and terrified nearly everyone. We also had an old collie with a long pointed snout. It used to follow Sam around. One day Sam was going for the dog food and the Alsatian in the shop came out and attacked our collie. Sam dropped the tin of dog food and went back to defend his pal. The Alsatian saw him coming and dashed straight through a little garden gate and up the stairs into the bedroom above the store. Sam went back, picked up his dog food and headed home with the collie.

I said to my wife, Madge, that we ought to train him to go over and collect the groceries, because I was convinced that in no time at all, if we gave him a bag or a basket in his mouth, with a note in it, he would definitely bring back anything we asked for.

But as I say, he had this habit of roving. One day both Sam and our collie disappeared. They were gone only about twenty minutes when the collie came back, but Sam wasn't with him. We never saw Sam after that.

Sam had been one of the easiest dogs to train I ever saw in my life. He probably met his death by being too friendly. He would walk up to anyone, wag his tail and look up as if to say, *How're you doing?*

At a certain point there was no use expecting him back. We searched bog holes and everywhere looking for him, just to bring him home, dead or alive, but we never found him.

It was right in a way, not to know exactly what happened to Sam. That way he might lunge through the door any minute, then shut it behind himself, as if to say, *Well, let's get on with it.*

Sometimes things end without ending, and Sam was like that. He didn't come back, and after a while we knew he couldn't.

A BRIDGE

OF SWANS

TESS
Why do stories start one place,
then end up entirely somewhere else?

JOSIE
Because the end is not at
the beginning.

Barnacle soup

Way back in the sixties, Madge, the children and I took our first and only holiday as a family. We went off down into Donegal and out on to Aranmore Island.

We rented a little house for something like four pounds a week. It was a funny island with the one narrow little road. You had to be very careful because some of the cars were bangers and unsafe, so you could be knocked down and end up in the ditch.

The island was police-free, and when they did come they were dependent on the natives to ferry them to the island. So the islanders always knew when the police were coming, and they sent word ahead. Then the pubs would close at the regular time, which was unusual. It also meant all cars would be pulled to the side of the road to avoid being ticketed.

I had four sons, David and Edmund, Ian and Malcolm, and they were fishing in the sea, standing on the rocks. This was the first time my family had ever fished in the sea. They weren't getting anything. So Madge and I went to the pub one night and began talking to this local man, an oldish fellow. We had the usual chat about our being on holiday and where did we come from. 'Oh,' he said, 'I guess it's your young fellas fishing off the shore.' 'That's right,' I said. 'But they're having no luck.'

'I'll tell you now,' he says, 'this is how you'll catch fish there. You send the boys down to pick a bucketful of barnacles and bring them back so you can boil them. Put them into a gallon can and, when you have them boiled, take the gallon of that soup to the shore and throw it into the sea. Keep back a few bits of the barnacles to bait the hooks, and with that you'll catch fish.'

So, with nothing better to do, we got the barnacles the next morning and boiled them. We made the gallon of soup and I went down to the sea and, boy, did I look ridiculous, throwing a gallon of soup into the broad Atlantic. If I stared out three thousand miles I could spot America. 'What in the name of God,' I said, 'will the difference of one gallon of barnacles make to this great Atlantic?'

Anyway, in she goes, a gallon of soup. Then I went off about my business and the boys set off fishing. When I came back two hours later, lo and behold, they had about six fish on the shore. One of them says to me, 'Here, you cast.' They were very young at the time and couldn't cast out far. So I took one of the spinning rods and cast it out a good bit. The bait had hardly touched the water when some rump of a fish hit it a wallop, and nearly tore the rod out of my hand, then took off, carrying bait and all.

It's possible the fish could smell the barnacle soup in the sea and it brought them in closer. Since the local man knew about it, it could possibly have been an old custom, handed down. But I didn't see any other lunatic with a gallon of soup, and I never saw the man afterward.

About a week later, towards the end of our stay, we were in bed and the humidity was so fierce it seemed you could die in such a bed with the heat. So Madge and I gave up sleep about two o'clock in the morning and decided to go somewhere. Since there were hardly any roads, we walked by moonlight across fields, climbed over stiles and stone walls, and walked up pathways until we landed at a pub where I'd heard there was music.

When we arrived, at about ten minutes past two, there was no music. We sat down at a table near an old man. Wouldn't he knock over the glass of rum he was drinking! Not only did he spill the rum, but he broke the glass. He was drunk, pure and simple. Up he went to the counter and he came back with another glass of rum and sat down.

I said to him, 'Sure, any fella can get drunk.'

'Drunk,' he says, 'I'm drunk this thirty years!' And, I believed him.

Anyway, I said to the barman, 'I thought you were having music tonight.'

'Ach,' he says, 'we're waiting for the band to come in from Burtonport.' Burtonport was the last town on the mainland, where you got the boat to come to the island.

At this stage it was half past two. We sat there and sure enough about four o'clock in the morning the band arrived, set up and started playing. So we listened and enjoyed ourselves until about nine o'clock. Then we went home again, across fields and over stiles, and had our breakfast with the family, with no one the wiser about our bed, empty from two in the morning, as we sat like two carefree people on a strange peaceful island and listened to music while dawn broke over the fields.

The pig factory

One of the enterprises my father took up when we were young was buying pigs. They would be killed and cleaned, then sold to a factory up in Derry where they were made into hams, bacon joints, rashers and sausage.

This meant on Monday mornings we'd be let off school to run messages the thirty yards from the slaughterhouse to the shop, taking the news of what each pig weighed to our mother, who would record it and pay the farmer. These farmers would be coming from the surrounding parishes with their pigs. There were few trucks or lorries in those times, so about forty carts and ponies would be lined up along the roadway.

We had a scale – a topless box with a door at either end – and each pig would be driven into it to be weighed. My father would employ five local men to kill the pigs. These men would hit the pigs with a steel mallet between their eyes, which knocked them out. Then they'd cut their throats and, within thirty to forty seconds, the pigs would have bled to death. Sometimes this blood was collected, and my mother and grandmother would make black pudding.

I remember one particular pig taking off out across the road, through a hedge, and up through a meadow – blood spewing out of him. Nobody seemed the least concerned about him getting away. They just went ahead with what they were doing and hardly gave him a glance. Then, about ten minutes later two men went mildly up the hill with a little trolley, put him on it and carried him back. He'd bled to death on his way to freedom, but at least he'd gone down with some brief notion of having escaped his fate. To this day I take that renegade pig as a sign that a blessing short-lived is still a blessing.

I remember another day this pig farmer warning

me, 'Young fellow, keep away from that horse because he'll bite you.' His pony was between the shafts of its cart and had the bit dropped out of its mouth eating hay.

But I forgot the warning. Next thing I knew I was caught on the shoulder by this horse's mouth. Luckily I was moving so fast he didn't have time to really clamp down, but he did mark my shoulder, front and back, with his teeth. I went around for a week with a strange tattoo on my shoulder, showing the boys where I'd narrowly escaped having the heart plucked out of me by a horse.

After the pigs were killed they were put into a big pot of boiling water so the hair could be scraped clean from them. Then they would be packed on to a lorry headed for Sligo. As it pulled away, you'd see forty-some pigs' feet hanging to each side, and if that lorry was passing a person on a bicycle, they could get a pig's foot in the snout or their teeth played like a timpani.

The carcasses were brought down to Sligo's railway station, loaded up and sent off to the North. This process went on, over and over, for five or six years, until the British put tariffs on goods coming into Northern Ireland from the South, and my father was once more driven out of business.

After that, my father became an agent for Russian oil in the West of Ireland. That lasted six years until the Second World War broke out and, since no Russian oil was then allowed into the country, that put an end to that. This state of affairs is what drove my father to the bogs to buy turf to supply fuel for boilers. Ireland was an isolated place where things got scarce. People and animals were starved out or plundered, or survived by their wits.

But going back to the time when pigs were our livelihood – now and again my brothers and I would be given a bladder from one of the newly slaughtered animals. We used to hang it up on a bush to dry and, depending on the weather, this could take two or more days. Next we'd pump it full of air.

A pig's bladder was soft enough to kick with bare feet, and since none of us wore shoes in summer, it made an ideal football. My brothers and I would thump it back and forth, uphill and down through the pastures until dark. When our father shouted us into the house, the bladder would be left where it fell.

There was one particular butcher, Jilly Mullens, who worked for our father, and if he happened upon our football, as he did more than once, he'd stab it with his knife, just for devilment. We usually had a spare bladder hidden in the hedge, so we'd just pump that up with a bicycle pump and start our game again.

This same butcher loved to castrate animals – rams and bulls and stallions. If he caught someone new to the whole procedure watching him, he'd throw the bloody testicles straight into their face. Then he'd laugh, splash this pint of Jeyes Fluid disinfectant on to the testicle bag of the animal, and pull the rope from the feet and neck of the creature so it could stand up again and take itself off into the field as if nothing much had happened to it.

Of course we knew better, and I remember watching such animals to see were they in pain, and imagining they probably were, but realising they weren't able to make a sign of it, which made it all the stranger – mute pain. I didn't know what to make of it and just did what the animals did – tried not to give it too much notice.

And out of it
he could not get

Mattie Reagan, in his young days, long before he came to us, lived in a backward place at the side of a mountain, and he would cross the hip of that mountain to go rambling at night. At the rambling house, six or seven of the locality would be gathered, and since there was no television in those days, people would sit and tell jokes and yarns, and smoke pipes until about midnight. Then they'd all go home in different directions.

Mattie knew the run to his home, same as

anybody knew the way to their own door. But it was an eerie sort of a night, coming back from the rambling house, and on his way home he found himself in this small garden, a field with a hedge around it. He knew there were gaps here and there, but he got into this field, and out of it he could not get. He walked it the entire night until daylight, before he could eventually see an opening in the hedge. He had passed that opening forty times, but he still couldn't get out. He reckoned it was the fairies had control of him.

That garden had a fairy fort in it. A fort is like an island in the middle of the land where people lived hundreds of years ago. You were never supposed to dig a hole or cut a bush in a fort. It's unlucky and, if you did it, you'd not live to a month past. Everybody knows where these forts are on their property. If you stand in one fort you can see at least three more from where you are. The people of those times had it arranged so that they could spread the alarm in case of intruders.

The reason you can't excavate or dig in a fort, I was told, is that it's also a graveyard. There were so many people living in the fort – it was only the size of a little garden – that they began inbreeding, and the children were dying. In those times, when such a child died without being baptised, they considered them unfit for heaven. They buried those dead babies outside the ring of the fort – that was one explanation why you weren't supposed to dig or excavate in, or even near a fort, and nobody would.

There was another thing: if you had a field with a lone tree in it, and the grass worn round it, you were not supposed to touch that either. A farmer, named Joe McKeown, built a new house. He and his family lived in the old house where he and his brothers and sisters had been born. Ten yards in front of that house, Joe and his wife built a brand-new two-storey house. To build, they had to cut a lone bush. After that, himself and his wife were dead within three years.

People said they met an early death because they'd cut that lone bush. Well, if you were told not to cut a branch off a certain tree, would you cut it? Joe didn't realise this was a lone bush he'd cut. You could make a mistake like that. There are more people who'll shake their heads to this day over Joe's sad mistake of cutting the lone bush.

Around some of those houses, when people died, lights used to appear. I heard several people talk about it. This light would come bouncing along the ground and it would circle a particular house. In that house, somebody would likely be very sick. But, after such a light appeared, within twenty-four hours, they'd be dead. I don't know if the light came when Joe McKeown died, but to this day that house lies empty.

Tommy Flynn and
his bealding

Tommy Flynn lived to be seventy years of age or more. He left a small cottage beside the lake where he had lived, and where we'd all visited him since we were young.

He was telling us one time how he'd been playing his fiddle about twenty miles from home. There were no cars, as it was during the First World War, so he cycled to this country house and he, along with a few more musicians, was playing the fiddle on a little platform in the corner of the kitchen while people were dancing.

'This particular woman kept looking up at me and winking,' he said. 'And I kept winking down at her.'

When the dance was over, Tommy stepped outside. It was a lovely August night and when he went over to pick up his bicycle, wasn't this woman waiting for him. So they set off cycling together, with the woman perched up before Tommy on the handlebars. Tommy pedals along the roadway and says to himself, *If I get a nice mossy bank, I'll lay this one down.*

I've forgotten to say that, even though he'd managed to play the fiddle that night, Tommy had this colossal lump at the side of his finger. It was a festered boil – a bealding. I think they were caused by bad nutrition.

So he got his mossy bank and he laid down the woman and started running his hand up between her legs. 'And when I got me hand just above the knee, didn't the One clap the two knees together and bursted me bealding!' This meant that, with the pain of it, Tommy could have no further interest in women that night.

Eventually he got in with this lassie from County Kildare. She was at least sixteen-stone weight and Tommy would have been about eight. Lucy was her name. She came on holidays and stayed with him three or four days or a week. Once we asked Tommy how he managed it, courting this big woman. Tommy owned a thirty-acre island with a hump in the middle. 'Be-Jee,' says Tommy, 'Lyin' on her is like lying' on the back of me island!'

Lucy worked for a hatchery that raised chickens. They were hatched from eggs, thousands of them, and sent all over Ireland. Her photograph was on the front of the box, looking as pleased as if she'd laid the eggs herself. Anyone who ever got a box of chickens from this hatchery would've had Lucy's photograph on that box for their mantelpiece. Maybe that's how Flynn got a notion of her.

Anyway, Lucy saw this big house down along the lake shore, and she said, 'If I'm going to stay with you, Tommy, I want a house just like that.' The prospects for this didn't look good to Tommy, so not long after this announcement, three or four of us got the job of bringing Lucy back to where she lived, and shortly thereafter we landed Tommy and her the hundred miles to Kildare.

Tommy got out in the town centre and waited while Lucy was saying goodbye to us. 'Goodbye Peter, goodbye Josie, goodbye Andy,' she says, giggling, and the next thing we knew she was back over to us again, spending ages saying goodbye to us all. And there was Flynn, standing like a heat-driven rush against the wall.

We'd told Tommy we'd give him exactly one hour and no more to court this woman. That's it, we said. So Tommy was wilting up against the wall and Lucy was saying goodbyes and goodbyes, when the next thing Tommy broke in and said, 'Lucy, come on, be-Jee, the hour is going!'

So off he went with this woman, and how they spent what was left of the hour, I don't know. But he never went near her after that. The romance broke off and word was she eventually married a farmer in Westmeath. She wanted too much from Tommy, who just wanted a simple life. But even so, women used to visit Tommy and take him places. He'd sit in front of his Stanley range day in and day out, and the women would go in and chat him. He could tell stories, morning, noon and night.

After Tommy's death the cottage got its own mind about things. The doors were falling off, the windows shattered, the whole place derelict for years. A strange kind of monument.

But eventually progress came and it was renovated entirely, white and shining, like a small castle hugging the roadway. If Tommy had come back he might feel he had to knock at his own door. Still, one night as I drove slowly past, I thought I heard fiddle music from out the back of the cottage. The stars were bright, the weather was fine, and my elbow was out the window.

Enigma

The year before my wife, Madge, died – while
we were doing reconstruction on the house
we called Moore's, on Lough Arrow – an overflow
pipe was diverted, and a hole the size of a cock's
egg was left in the gable.

Later, during my second spring alone in the
house, I was walking around outside when I saw a
little swallow go straight into that hole near the
roof. Then I noticed there were two birds. I
realised they were going to build a nest, which
would mean noise over my head every night and
morning. I waited until I thought the birds had
gone out during the day, then up I went with a

little trowel and cement, and plugged the hole.

About a day or two later, I happened to be walking around the back of the house when I heard scratching and little claws running up and down inside the fascia board. One of the birds must have been trapped. So I got the stepladder, a hammer and chisel, and climbed up.

I opened the hole only about two inches, when out flew the swallow. Suddenly, from the very top of the house this other bird took off, straight after it.

That bird, the male, had sat for nearly the whole time, probably two days, waiting for his little friend to be released. The bird I had freed hadn't gone a hundred yards until the male was straight in behind her, and the two of them disappeared down over the lake.

About the same time, house martins built on the gables. One nest was over the back door in the V of the roof. The result was that, since they cleaned out the nest every day, there was always an offering on the step in the morning, and you could get anointed, going in or out the door.

One day in the middle of summer I noticed that the second nest, which was above the windows to the bedroom, for some unknown reason, was being attacked by about twenty or more birds, and bit by bit, in seconds, they literally demolished it before my eyes.

Such a flurry of activity you never saw. But they didn't disturb the house martins' nest over the door, and I often wonder why they decided to smash and pull apart one nest, yet completely ignore the other.

I had been told it was very lucky for house martins to build on your house. But they built only that one year, the year after Madge's death, then destroyed one nest and left the other. Even though the nest they spared still hung over the back door, no birds ever made a home of it again.

I knew for a long time the nest would never be used, but I kept up hope, letting it be. It was as if the sorrow of the house had driven even the birds away.

Finally, there was no denying it: they had abandoned my house. One day I took a shovel and knocked down the remaining nest.

A bridge of swans

One night in August, I was leaving a dance in the countryside, and it so happened that a young nurse, whose sister I knew, was also leaving at the same time. We each had bicycles and we cycled along the road together for several miles.

There was a full moon, and when we'd cycled about four miles, we came to Lough Skean, where we stopped and put our feet up on the low wall above the lake and looked down. Right under us were four swans. We admired those white swans in the moonlight awhile and then went on.

Years later I was telling a woman in Sligo about seeing the swans with Madge when we were young, before we courted and she became my wife. How we'd loved looking down at those swans on that first, moonlit night.

The woman happened to attend Madge's funeral on the shores of another lake, Lough Arrow, which also has swans. 'Did you hear the swans in the bay?' she asked me. 'They were calling to each other all during the service,' she said.

This made me remember the first night I'd met Madge, how the swans were chirping and cackling in the bay that night. And so, when we'd buried her in Ballindoon, the swans had been at the same thing.

Something passed over me when I was told about the cries of the swans at the funeral, as if our first night was suddenly joined to our last day, the day I was burying her.

For a moment Madge came back to me – a beautiful young girl with a bicycle in the moonlight. But the strange thing was, I couldn't hear the swans that day. The woman heard them for me. I was deaf as a spade myself at the funeral.

Acknowledgements

Grateful acknowledgement is made to the editors and publishers of the following publications: *Artful Dodge*: 'A fiddle in the boat', 'Tommy Flynn and his bealding', 'A mouse on the shoe', 'A stray bullet and sick cattle', 'A blind tongue', 'A wild hand' and 'An Irish solution'; *Bellingham Review*: 'A fox and a one-legged goose' and 'Barnacle soup'; *Double Take*: 'A lake in the boat' and 'The rate inspector'; *Hayden's Ferry Review*: 'A hare on the chest', 'A wheelbarrow on the bog', 'And out of it he could not get' and 'The best blood in Europe'.

I wish to thank Tess Gallagher, who listened to these stories, and tirelessly revised them with me over twelve years.

ACKNOWLEDGEMENTS

Many thanks to Dorothy Catlett, who took the stories off the tapes Tess made, typing and retyping them as we made changes.

Dermot Healy gave substantial and inspired help to the book at a formative stage.

The fine artwork created especially for the book by Anne M. Anderson is an excellent complement to the stories, and Tess and I thank her for it.

Thanks also to those who heard stories from this collection, or read them in manuscript form, and made suggestions – especially Eileen McDonagh, Ciaran Carson, Dan Bourne, Mike Silverstein and Kari Harinaka, Bill Stull and Maureen Carroll, Greg Simon, Alan and Joyce Rudolph, our wonderful Blackstaff team – Patsy Horton, Janice Smith and Cormac Austin – and my childhood friend, Paddy Hunt, who encouraged me, before he passed on, to tell more stories about my own life.

JOSIE GRAY
AUTUMN 2007